SCOOBY-DOO

Story Adaptations by Etta Wilson
Illustrations by Bob Singer
Art Direction by Linda Karl

MALLARD PRESS
An Imprint of BDD Promotional Book Company, Inc.
666 Fifth Avenue
New York, N.Y. 10103

"Mallard Press and its accompanying design and logo
are trademarks of BDD Promotional Book Company, Inc."

Copyright © 1990 Hanna-Barbera Productions, Inc.
© 1990 Universal City Studios, Inc.
Jetsons ® property © 1990 Hanna-Barbera Productions, Inc.
First published in the United States of America in
1990 by The Mallard Press.

Story Adaptations by March Media, Inc.
Illustrations by Singer/Bandy Group
Produced by Hamilton Projects, Inc.

ISBN 0-792-45151-1

Printed in the United States

MALLARD
PRESS

What A Night for A Knight

Scooby-Doo and his friends Shaggy, Velma, Daphne, and Freddy were walking home from the movie. The moon was full and it was a nervous night! Suddenly they spotted a pickup truck sitting in the road ahead.

"Rhuts rat?" barked Scooby.

"Look! There's an empty old suit of black armor in the driver's seat," said Freddy.

"Maybe he went out for the night! Get it?" Shaggy's joke didn't seem too funny to anybody but Scooby. There was a tag on a large crate in the back of the truck. It said:

Professor J. Hyde-White, Archaeologist
London, England
Deliver to the County Museum

"So that's where this knight was headed for," Velma said.

"Yes, but where's the professor?" asked Daphne.

"Looks like another mystery to solve!"

"Right!" said Scooby.

They started looking for clues at the museum. The man in charge, Mr. Wikles, didn't seem very happy that they had found the Black Knight. He said it was not a good time for the professor to be delivering the armor from England— because of the legend.

"What legend?" asked Freddy.

"The Black Knight is supposed to come alive when the moon is full."

"Wow! The moon was full last night!" said Shaggy.

On the way out of the museum, Scooby stopped to investigate something.

"Scooby-Doo, where are you?" called Daphne.

Scooby barked and ran to catch up. He was wearing some strange glasses, and no one knew what they were.

"There's one way to find out!" said Freddy.

At the library they read that the special glasses were used by archaeologists and were only made in England. Now they were sure something fishy was going on at the museum.

5

That night they went back to the museum. It was locked up tighter than a drum, but thin-man Shaggy found a way in — with help from a ladder and a jack.

Once they were all inside, they decided to split up to look for the professor.

"You stand guard, Scooby," said Freddy.

"Uh, Uh. . .Uh, Uh!" Scooby didn't want to be alone in the dark museum.

"Would you do it for a Scooby Snack?" Freddy asked.

Scooby couldn't say no! "Slurp, chomp, gulp!"

Velma and Shaggy hadn't gone far until they realized they were being followed — by Scooby! The three of them started through the dark rooms. Shaggy pulled the shade on the window to keep out the bright moon. Then he took a wrong turn!

"Oh, no! We lost Shaggy," cried Velma.

Scooby's teeth began to chatter.

As Velma and Scooby were searching for Shaggy, Scooby happened to look behind him — the Black Knight! Scooby took off fast and knocked Velma to the floor.

"Now look what that dog did. He knows I can't see without my glasses!"

The Black Knight couldn't see very well either. When he tripped over Velma, he landed on his face in a trap.

Scooby had found the best room of all. It was full of bones!

"Sniff. Scooby-Dooby-Doo. . .Slurp!"

Scooby was enjoying the great pile of bones until he heard moans. He thought the Black Knight had found him. Time to run!

In the gallery Shaggy saw a picture missing from the wall. He was sure the Black Knight was walking around just as the legend said, and called everyone to help him check the clue.

Then Daphne found something else.

"Is that blood on the floor?" she asked.

"No, it's paint—and it leads down the hall," said Freddy.

The trail of paint ended at the mummy case. And behind the case was a secret room! It was very messy with lots of paintings, some of them only half done.

"Look! There are two paintings exactly alike!"

"Right, Velma," said Freddy.   "This just about solves the mystery!"

"Rit does???" barked Scooby.

They started out the back to call the sheriff, but Daphne picked the wrong door. Time to run again!

14

In the relic room, Shaggy and Scooby hid in an old biplane. When the plane started, Scooby decided to be the pilot, and the chase was on. Now it was the Black Knight who was running away!

The plane caught him. As the Knight's helmet fell off, they saw he was not a knight at all.

It was Mr. Wikles!

The sheriff arrived, and Freddy, Velma, Shaggy, and Daphne put all the clues together. Mr. Wikles was part of a gang who stole the real paintings from the museum and put up fake ones. They had to get rid of the professor because he would have spotted the fakes.

"Oh, my gosh!" said Daphne. "We never found Professor Hyde-White."

"Rook! Rook!" Scooby barked.

"It's Scooby-Doo with a shoe!" said Velma.

Scooby led them straight to the Professor. He was explaining how Wikles had made up the legend about the Black Knight when they saw the suit of armor move.

"Zoinks! He's alive!" exclaimed Shaggy.

But it was Scooby having the last laugh on his friends.

"Scooby-Dooby-Doo!"

Scooby Gumbo

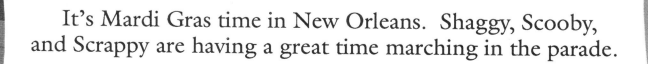

It's Mardi Gras time in New Orleans. Shaggy, Scooby,
and Scrappy are having a great time marching in the parade.

"This is great Dixieland jazz, eh, guys?" Shaggy asked.

"Reah, Razz!" barked Scooby.

"Hey, Uncle Scooby, look up there." Scrappy had spotted a French restaurant on the street ahead.

"Like, New Orleans seafood . . . sounds good to me," said Shaggy.

"Right!" Scooby was all for eating.

At the table on the sidewalk, they were greeted by the French chef.

"Bonjour. Your order please?" Then he took a close look at Scooby and Scrappy. "We do not serve zee dogs zere!" he said.

"Rogs? Rhere?" asked Scooby.

"Oud! Get oud!" the chef roared and kicked all three of them out of the restaurant.

"You big meanie!" yelled Scrappy. "You can't do that to my Uncle Scooby. Let's go back in there and eat!"

"Raggy, rook!" Scooby saw something very interesting across the street — a wig shop.

"Hey, Scrappy, come on," called Shaggy. "I've got an idea. Where's there a wig, there's a way!"

Soon they were back at the restaurant, looking very different.

"Give us three orders of shrimp creole," ordered Shaggy.

"As you wish, monsieur," said the chef. He started for the kitchen without a word about not serving dogs. The wigs had worked!

"Hey, I wonder what this thing does." Scrappy pulled on the arm of a diving suit beside the door. When the suit made a growling noise, Scrappy was ready to fight!

"Rappy-Roo!" barked Scooby.

"Don't worry, Uncle Scooby. I can handle him!"

Scrappy twisted the helmet of the suit so hard, it flew through the air — right onto the chef's head as he came from the kitchen!

"Someone will pay for zis!" he yelled.

"Zoinks! Like, run!" called Shaggy.

They found a place to hide on a float in the parade, but the chef was right behind them.

"Dogs! There you are! I'll get you!" he shouted as he climbed on the float.

The three friends slipped into a band on the sidewalk. Scooby played the biggest instrument in the band — and tried to hide at the same time.

"Let's make it snappy, Scoob. Get it?" laughed Shaggy. "Reah!"

"Gotcha!" The chef had found them and he was very mad! "Zere ees no place to hide!"

Scooby suddenly stopped beating out a jazz tune on the big drum, and it rolled right over the chef!

There was just enough time for Shaggy, Scooby, and Scrappy to run into a big room and block the door with bags of sugar.

"Whew! We're safe now, Scoob!"

"Right, Raggy!"

"Yezz, in my kitchen!" It was the chef!

"Let's split, Scoob! Head for cover! Quick, Scrappy!" called Shaggy.

From one stew pot to the next, the chef chased the three around and around the kitchen. "I'll feex you!" he yelled.

Then Scrappy found the mixer.

"I'll fix that mean old chef with a batch of my special sticky, scrappy gumbo!"

He poured some of everything on the counter into the mixing bowl and flipped the switch. The gumbo was ready to serve just as the chef slipped on a pile of sugar beside the counter!

"Slurp! Slurp! What is zis?" The chef liked what he tasted. "This gives me an idea! I still do not allow dogs in my restaurant, but zey are welcome in my kitchen!"

"Ruh?" asked Scooby.

A short while later everyone was busy in the kitchen.

"Okay, Uncle Scooby, I'm ready to decorate the cupcakes we baked," Scrappy called.

"That Scrappy is some pastry chef, Scoob, but it looks like you're for dessert." Shaggy laughed.

"Reah, Slurp, slurp. Scooby-Dooby-Doo!"

Scooby-Doo Finds The Clue

Scooby and his friends Shaggy, Freddy, Daphne, and Velma were at Rocky Point Beach for a night-time beach party — in spite of reports about mysterious events.

"Wow! I can already taste those chocolate-covered hot dogs!" said Shaggy.

"Yuck! Your stomach must be made of scrap iron," Velma replied.

"Where is Scooby-Doo?" Freddy asked. "I haven't seen him since we unloaded the Mystery Machine."

"He went surfing," said Daphne as they danced.

35

Out on the surfboard, Scooby had bumped into something strange. "Ripes!" barked Scooby. "Zoinks!" yelled Shaggy. "It's a sea-going ghost!!"

The whole gang ran up the beach to hide behind some rocks. Scooby ran the fastest!

"There's something mighty spooky going on here," said Daphne.

"Right!" Velma said. "The newspaper reported that boats vanish on this beach and the sheriff can't find them."

"Maybe the old beach hermit, Ebenezer Shark, can give us a clue. Let's pay him a visit — tonight," said Freddy.

Ebenezer Shark was sure that Scooby and his friends had seen the ghost of Captain Cutler.

"How do you know it was Captain Cutler?" Freddy asked.

"Because his boat was wrecked on a foggy night like this. It ran into one of those fancy yachts and sent Captain Cutler down to the graveyard of ships. But his ghost always moves through the fog just before the boats vanish."

Shark stopped talking as they heard growls and snarls coming from the cellar.

"Hey, it's Scooby," said Daphne.

"Zoinks! He's got that ghost again!" Shaggy yelled.

"Oh, no," said Shark, "that's my old diving suit. Now if you want to know more about Cutler, you'd better see his wife up at the old lighthouse."

"Ol righthouse?" Scooby gulped.

Velma, Shaggy, and Scooby went inside the creepy lighthouse.

"It looks like she practices witchcraft," said Velma.

Just then Shaggy felt long skinny fingers on his shoulder. It was widow Cutler.

"We think we saw the ghost of Captain Cutler tonight," Velma said to the old woman.

"Aye, you did," she replied. "I brought him back from the grave with my witchcraft, but I should have left him under the sea. Now he's made another yacht vanish to get revenge for his wreck."

"Let's get out of this scary pad," Shaggy whispered to Velma.

MAGIC
MADE EASY

Out on the beach, they saw a strange glow coming from a drain pipe. Velma and Shaggy pushed Scooby in to investigate. In minutes he was back with his mouth full.

"Like, Wow! Glowing seaweed!" said Shaggy.

"That seaweed is found only in the graveyard of ships below the water," Velma said. "That's where Captain Cutler went down and that's where we'll find the answer to our mystery!"

"Well, Scooby-Dooby-Doo!" barked Scooby.

Scooby and the gang dressed in scuba diving suits. Soon they were on a boat headed out to sea.

"Look, there's one of the yachts from the marina," said Daphne. "And it's moving toward that cove."

"But there's no one on board," Freddy pointed out.

"What's making it go?" asked Freddy.

"Ghost power!" Velma replied.

"Well, like I always say — onward and downward — to the graveyard of ships, that is," said Freddy.

When they dived below the water, they split into two teams to look for the ghost. Shaggy and Scooby swam toward one of the old sunken ships. They didn't know they were being watched.

"Raggy, rook!" barked Scooby. He had found glowing footprints on the ocean floor.

"Okay, Scoob, let's follow them inside the ship, but back to back so we don't get surprised!" said Shaggy.

In the dark cabin of the ship it was hard to see.

"Scooby-Doo, Scooby-Doo, where are you?" called Shaggy.

"I round a rue, Raggy! I round a rue!"

"A clue, Scooby? Zoinks! It's scuba tanks — all ready for use! Let's find the gang quick."

Shaggy and Scooby swam out to tell Freddy, Daphne, and Velma about the scuba tanks. Then Daphne spotted more glowing footprints.

"Those footprints vanish right into the side of the cliff," said Velma. "Now what do we do?"

"Like, rest — I'm pooped!" Shaggy sat on a nearby rock. Suddenly a door in the cliff opened to a secret passage.

"Shaggy, you're a genius!" Freddy said. "Come on gang, let's follow his trail."

At the end of the secret passage, Scooby and the gang found a giant hidden cavern full of yachts.

"Look, there's the yacht we saw disappear in the cove, and it's tied to a mini-sub," said Daphne.

"Things are beginning to add up," Freddy said. "And I've got a plan."

He put a bar of soap in a spray container, attached it to a fire hose on one of the boats and turned on the water. Instant suds!

"Okay, Shaggy, start the noisemaker."

When the ghost came down the ramp, he slipped in the suds and fell right into Scooby's net. The glowing ghost was trapped.

"Now let's see who our mystery ghost is," said Freddy.
Velma pulled off the helmet. "Who is it?" she asked.

"I got it!" said Shaggy. "Does this piece of seaweed remind you of that picture on widow Cutler's wall?"

"It's Captain Cutler!" cried Daphne and Velma.

"And he's been stealing the yachts from the marina with that mini-sub, but everyone thought he was dead at sea," said Freddy. "He was covered with that glowing seaweed when he stored the extra scuba tanks in the sunken ship."

"Well, that wraps up the mystery — thanks to Scooby's clues!" said Shaggy.

"Scooby-Dooby-Doo!"